The Ghost

First published in Great Britain in 2025 by Black Shuck Books

All content © Terry Grimwood 2024

Cover design by WHITEspace
from "At the Ferdinandsbrücke, Vienna"
Photographer unknown
Courtesy of the Wien Museum Collection

Set in Caslon by WHITEspace
www.white-space.uk

978-1-917173-04-9

The Ghost

by
Terry Grimwood

BLACK
SHUCK
BOOKS

"If we leave the world stage in disgrace, we'll have lived for nothing"

Adolf Hitler, 25th April 1945

Her baby. Crying. The baby she clutches to herself. She, in turn, is the woman Slavko holds close to himself. He is behind her, his knife to her throat. The woman's eyes are wide, her face ashen and locked into an expression of fear so absolute, so all-consuming, that it devours her humanity. She is an animal caught in a trap. She is prey in the jaws of a predator.

She is pretty, that much I can see, dark-haired and dark-eyed. But, like everyone in this filthy back street, like those cowering in the doorways on either side, she is poor and dirty and worn down by the grindstone that is life here.

Her baby shrieks. It doesn't understand. It is a near-mindless bundle of needs and hungers. Its mother understands though. She feels the sharpness of the blade. It has broken her skin. She can feel the warmth of her own blood as it runs from the wound and down her throat to stain her ragged, grubby dress.

I see it all clearly, despite the inconstant gas lamps and the near-useless yellow-orange glow that spills, furnace-like, from cracked, dirty windows and open doors of the surrounding houses. Oh yes, I see it all clearly, sighted along the short barrel of my police revolver.

Heavy it is, in my trembling hands, heavy and lethal. Slavko's forehead is my target. But I must allow for the gun's kick, which will jerk the barrel upwards. It means that if I don't lower my aim slightly, the bullet will pass over his head and the woman will surely die.

So, I force my hands and my aching arms to lower the weapon, slowly, carefully, until it is in line with the woman's left eye. Too low? I don't know. But I must do something. She is bleeding. The baby is screaming.

God forgive me.

I slowly, gently, squeeze the trigger.

The shot is a detonation that splits the world in two...

VIENNA 1911

One

I walk through the anonymous corridors of a hospital. I have no wish to be here. A baby is crying. The sound spirals from out of a nearby ward and drives through my aching skull like a chisel into a brick wall. No one, none of the white-starched nurses or hurrying doctors here, pays it any mind. The sound is harsh and discordant. I want it to stop. I want the little brat to shut up.

It is the child of a patient or a visitor, I suppose. Whichever it is, someone in this wretched house of sickness needs to make it *stop*.

Surely I am not alone in my hatred of hospital wards. Surely others loathe the white walls, the gleaming white tiles, the white coats of the doctors, the crisp uniforms and white headdresses worn by the nurses. This is how I imagine death to be. White nothingness.

There is the smell too, of course, that unbearable chemical stink, underlain with the tang of excrement. No matter where you pack human beings together, they will soon stink. It reminds me of opening a cell door in the gendarmerie headquarters on a prisoner who has spent a night of free board with us.

Ah, this is the ward, the name given to me, reluctantly, by one Dr Weis.

I enter and cross to the bed of the man I have come to see.

I am shaken by him.

Yes me, a police detective, unnerved by this insignificant, wretched-looking specimen lying there in his borrowed bed. It is, of course, my own idiocy that has made me afraid of this human shadow. But I am unnerved nonetheless.

"Herr Heidler?" I say by way of greeting.

"Hitler," the patient says. His voice is a growl. "My name is Hitler, not so difficult to remember, is it?"

He is… ah, I cannot describe him. Mad, perhaps? No, not exactly. Intense, yes, that is it. Physically he is nondescript, pale, undernourished. His flesh is grey. His skinny carcass held motionless on the bed by pain. A sour smell curls outwards from his dirt-grimed skin.

He wears a hospital gown. His sunken chest is wrapped in a bandage. The bullet narrowly missed his heart and lungs, according to Doctor Weis. A lucky shot, for him. Unlucky, presumably, for his would-be assassin. Ribs have been broken, on his left side. Skin and muscle torn and burned. There has been bleeding and shock, but the man will survive, providing there is no infection.

He stares at me. Into me. Through me.

"Forgive me," I say. I don't feel like talking. I want a cigarette. I need a drink. "Your name has been misspelled on this report. Now. Let me see, your Christian name is Adolphus, yes?"

A nod.

"No other names?"

"No. Adolphus is my only name."

I introduce myself. "Leutnant Graf, of the Vienna Gendarmerie's Special Detective Service."

A grunt. He is not interested.

I press on. "I have been charged with finding out who shot you, and why." A mundane sort of case for a detective from the Special Service. A gentle start back to my duties after the Slavko incident.

"We all have enemies," Hitler says. He turns that stare on me again. I try not to flinch. I want to press my fingertips against my throbbing temples, but resist.

"All of us?"

"Are you that blind?" Hitler seems energised now.

No, I am not blind. This is a troubled city. "Enlighten me," I say. "Open my eyes. Who are *your* enemies, Herr Hitler?"

"The same as yours Herr Leutnant. The Serbians and Jews who infest Vienna like a disease, and the socialists who want to bring anarchy."

"It seems that we have lot of enemies, you and I."

"Are you making fun of me?" There is no smile. There is no hint that this man has any sense of humour whatsoever.

"No, but I would like you to be more specific."

"I don't know who it was, but I do know why."

"You do?"

"There are those who work to undermine our nation, enemies who work for its downfall and the downfall of Germany."

"Germany?"

"Our great ally."

I take a breath and regret it immediately, because the breath is laden with those smells of disease and healing that I hate so much. The man is either suffering from shock or he is deranged. His unfocussed meanderings are no help whatsoever. His antisemitism and racialism are deep, but not so unusual in Vienna.

"Where do you live?" I ask. Time to change direction. Time for specifics.

"The Men's Dormitory in Meldemannstrasse."

I have heard of it, a source of great civic pride is that hostel. "And work?"

"I am an artist."

"Really?"

"Oh, so *you* also refuse to believe me."

"Also?"

"Those idiots at the Academy. Three times they have rejected me. *Three* times. They accept others, the incompetents, dabblers and daubers, but not me. Never me."

"So, you paint for a living?"

"Yes. I told you that, didn't I?" He seems to dissolve into the pillow.

"Please." A voice from behind me. Startled, I turn to see that Dr Weis is back. The man is a ghost, almost as grey and pale as his patient. I pity him for having to care for this brute.

"One moment," I tell him.

"No, Herr Leutnant, you cannot—"

"Adolphus," I say. "Did you get into a fight? Was there a brawl or an argument? You must tell me what happened?"

He opens his burning blue eyes and glares up at me. "No fight." He sighs and shuts his eyes again.

"Adolphus. Wake up. Adolph—"

His eyes flicker open again. "One man…from the shadows…Serbian…Jew… one only…"

This man, this Adolphus Hitler, is not going to be much help in the apprehension of his attackers. I'm glad of an excuse to get away from him. He is dirty. He smells bad. There is fire in his eyes and darkness in his voice. I am imagining it, of course, but nonetheless, he disturbs me.

Captain Brunner will tell me that it is because I am not ready for duty. He thinks I may never be ready.

15

Two

I return to the scene of the crime, the Vienna State Opera House. The grey afternoon air is cold and heavy with snow. I relish it as I stand on the opposite side of the road to the building's façade. I breathe deeply, trying to clear stink of the hospital from my lungs.

The opera house itself is as magnificent as the name suggests. Trams trundle by. Each one briefly obscures its grandeur, as if to remind me that such ancient splendour is slowly, but steadily, being pushed into the background by the new and brash. I stare up at the statues in their ornate alcoves above the main entrance, mute witnesses to last evening's violence.

It seems that no one who was here saw or heard anything more than the flash of a muzzle and the sharp report of a gunshot. Some glimpsed one man running away as another crumpled to the ground. It was dark. It was busy. Trams, carriages and people.

I hurry across the road to the spot where Hitler the operagoer fell bleeding and screaming to the pavement. His blood is still visible. A dark stain that will soon be eradicated by the coming snow. People skirt round it. Many look down, puzzled or repulsed. The opera house looms over the me, an intimidating confection of glamour, light and opulence. I cannot reconcile the image of Hitler entering this place with his worn-out suit and long hair.

I take a stroll. There are shops and great buildings on either side, but few alleyways or side streets from which an assailant could emerge. He must have hidden in the evening crowds, revealing himself as an assassin at the last moment. A panicked shot, one that was not immediately fatal and probably not fatal at all. I try to imagine his fear, the hard beat of his heart. The weight of the revolver, hidden inside a jacket or coat. The moment comes. Shaking, oh he would be shaking all right, he squeezes the trigger: explosion, flash, the jolt of the weapon in his fist. The upward jerk of its recoil. An instant of nothing. An instant of waiting. Ears already ringing, all other sound—

even the baby's cries

—smothered.

Then an impact—

blood, burned hair, an eruption of skull fragments and gobs of brain…

—Adolphus Hitler crumples and falls.

Finally comes realisation that you have turned a healthy, able human being into a bloody mess. You have injured, perhaps even killed them. It doesn't matter who your victim is, or what they are about to do—

The knife falls and the woman staggers forwards to her knees as Slavko is thrown backwards. He doesn't cry out. He dies in the moments it takes for the bullet to drill through his forehead and explode out of the back of his skull.

—you have inflicted pain and destruction, but *you* are also wounded. Your own wound is less bloody, but every bit as deep as theirs.

Pulling myself together, I turn and explore the street in the opposite direction.

I feel utterly alone at that moment and realise that this is the longest I have been outside on the street, and the longest I have spent away from my apartment, since I killed Slavko. Much of that time is lost in an alcoholic haze, a timeless fog in which, at some unremembered point, my beloved Adela walked out of our rooms for the last time. I cannot blame her. She no longer had a man worthy of being called husband. She is free to find better. I miss her though. My God, how I miss her.

There are people out, most of them in a hurry to reach whatever destination they seek and find warmth. They are shapes. They are disconnected from me and I from them. I wonder if they even see me. If I reached out to touch any of them, would my hand pass straight through their flesh as if they were a ghost?

No, *I* am the ghost.

We of the Special Detective Service are trained to use firearms because it is expected that we will encounter armed opponents and be forced to engage them, but a wooden target does not breathe. It has no beating heart. It does not stare into your eyes and plead for its life, and it does not die.

Three

The Men's Dormitory on Meldemannstrasse 27 is in the Brigittenau district. I am startled by its size and imposing demeanour. I had expected some tumbledown hall or tenement, but this is an enormous edifice that resembles a lakeside schloss.

It is growing dark. Lights shine from many of the windows on the lower storeys, of which I count six. I knock and show my identification to the doorman before I can be mistaken for a prospective resident. The duty manager is called. He is a fussy little man with a neatly curled moustache and hair elaborately combed so as to cover his encroaching baldness. His suit is immaculate, complemented by a watch chain stretched across his ample belly. Beaming with forced good humour and pride he leads me up a single flight of somewhat utilitarian stairs to the comfortable main office. The room is more study than workplace. He invites me to sit in either of the plush armchairs that face the heavy oak desk. The fire burning in the grate indicates that he has already settled himself in for a peaceful night's work.

"We have electric light and steam heating," he says proudly. "There are workshops here, a communal mess room, and a sitting room. Oh, and of course we have the bathrooms where we scrub and de-louse the men before they take up residence. Cleanliness is next to Godliness, is it not, Herr Leutnant."

"Who are your residents?" I ask.

"Anyone who is down on their luck and can pay for a bed. Two-and-a-half krona, that is all we ask. Many are workers who have come into Vienna from the countryside but cannot afford a room. Others are men who have fallen on bad times. We even have university professors here. We can accommodate 515 men. Imagine that, Herr Leutnant, 515 men who do not have to sleep on the streets of our city."

I am impressed. I try not to be. I am, after all, a police officer and, therefore, required to be world-weary. "Who built this place?"

"It is a work of philanthropists. I understand that the Rothschilds contributed a great deal."

"The Roth..." I chuckle. How can I not? The vehemently anti-semitic Adolphus Hitler is being given a place to sleep by Jewish benefactors.

"I assume that you are here because of Adolphus. I hear that he was shot and wounded on the street."

"You know him? Personally? I mean there are 500—"

"515."

"*515* residents. I didn't think you'd know them all by name."

"Most of them, I do not, but Adolphus..." He shakes his head. "He is a troublemaker. He is rude, noisy and argues with anyone who disagrees with him. However," the duty manager shrugs, "he pays his board and so is entitled to stay here."

"Disagrees with him? About what?"

"Anything. You'll have to ask the other residents. I try to stay out of his way."

"Do you know anything else about him? Something that would be helpful to us?"

"He is lazy and disorganised. He was on his last legs when he came here. One of the convents took him in, originally. He was sleeping rough, you see. He works, sometimes. He shovels snow and carries sacks of coal at the railway station. Oh, and he paints pictures and sells them. He spends most of the money he earns on the opera – Wagner, that's his music. Too long-winded and noisy for me, but he can't seem to get his fill of it."

I am shown into the large, plain lounge. There is a smell I remember from my training days. It is the perfume of barracks and academies where men live in close proximity; cigarettes, sweat and coffee. A large, somewhat institutional-looking clock hangs on one wall. It ticks with irritating loudness, the sound overlaid with muted conversation. There are about twenty men in here at the moment. Some look truly down-at-heel, others are better dressed. The men sit around in armchairs and at tables, playing cards or chess, and reading newspapers or books. Some write. A thin pall of tobacco smoke mists the room.

The manager leaves me. I cough for attention and hold up my identification card. "Who here knows Adolphus Hitler?"

"We all do," a large, glowering man growls from a chair on the far side of the room. "What of it?" The man applies a match to an elaborate meerschaum. He puffs and frowns even more deeply as the pipe refuses to draw.

"He was shot and wounded last night, outside the State Opera House."

"Ah, that was probably someone trying to put a stop to those bloody Rhinemaidens and their interminable warbling," the glowering man said. There was general laughter. "He must have missed and hit Dolf instead."

"Dolf never stops talking about Wagner," says another man, this one slight built, almost completely bald. He lays down his book. "Come to that, he never stops talking about anything."

Dolf must be a nickname. I can't imagine that it meets with Hitler's approval.

"Do any of you have any idea who would want to shoot him?"

"Most of us in here," the bald man says, and there is more laughter.

"Ah, he's all right," the glowering man says. "He generally keeps himself to himself. He spends most of his time in the work room, painting those bloody pictures of his."

"He works from here?"

"This isn't a doss house." The glowering man sounds offended. "A lot of us work, me included. We've hit hard times, that's all. This is a respectable establishment."

"You said that all of you in here would like to shoot him—" I hastily quell their frightened protests. "It's all right, please. I realise you were joking, but none of you seem to like him."

The bald man shrugs. "Like Franz said, he keeps himself to himself. It's just that once he decides to talk, you can't shut him up. If anyone disagrees with him, he yells and screams like a spoilt child. It used to be funny. I used to annoy him on purpose, just to see him go mad. I used to say, 'That Wagner, he's Jewish you know'. He always bit, like a fish on a hook. But I'm tired of it now."

There are general murmurs of agreement.

"You want to see his cubicle?" the glowering man, Franz, says and leads the way upstairs.

Hitler's cubicle is spartan enough. There is little in the way of personal possessions in here. There are no ornaments or photographs. His bed is unmade. His painting tools – a jar of brushes, a palette, a pile of paper and several postcards – sit atop a small cabinet by the bed. I pick up one of the pictures. It is a watercolour recreation of the Hofburg. I select another, which shows the Albertina Gallery. Each is an exact copy of the photographs on the postcards. They are well executed. Hitler does appear to have a talent, but it is unexceptional.

"How does he sell these?" I ask, and it is at that moment that I notice something odd about the pictures. They seem cold and soulless. It triggers another memory, of when I told him who I was and how disinterested he had been. Again, I feel unease, a sense that everything is wrong, that two unmatching pieces of a jigsaw puzzle have been forced together.

"...a friend who does it for him." Franz is saying.

"A friend?"

"Yes, he sells them on, to a Jew art dealer." Franz chuckles ruefully. "Somewhat ironic, don't you think, seeing as Dolf doesn't like Jews very much?"

"That's not unusual in this city," I say.

"They don't bother me. Everyone's the same as far as I'm concerned. We have a few in here. Pleasant enough. Can't see what the fuss is about."

"Who is this friend?"

"His name is Fritz Walter. He lives here a lot of the time. Bit of a shyster, if you ask me, but he's the nearest thing Dolf has to a friend, although the pair of them seem to have fallen out lately. Not that Dolf ever argues with anyone. He talks. You listen." Franz pauses and fiddles with his pipe. His tone softens. "How badly is he hurt? I mean, he's an odd one, but he doesn't deserve to be shot."

"I think he'll survive."

Franz nods. "Good. Tell him we all wish him well when you next speak to him."

"I will," I lie.

Satisfied that I have harvested all I can from this particular crop of Hitler's associates, I bid them good evening and see myself down to the front entrance. I nod another good evening to the doorman as I pass. He lifts his hand in a lazy acknowledgment and returns his attention to his pipe, newspaper and stove.

The front door opens. There is a gust of icy air. A figure steps in from the dark, muffled in a coat and scarf. I glimpse snow, framed in the doorway behind him. The doorman calls out to him; "Good evening Herr Walter."

"Walter?" I address the newcomer. "Fritz Walter?"

The man stops in his tracks. "Who wants to know?"

Out comes my identification. "Leutnant Graf of the Special Detective Department."

Walter's eyes widen in alarm, then he spins about and runs.

I am outside in a moment. I see him stumbling and slipping along the pavement to my right. People cry out as he blunders past. Someone falls. The ground is slippery. Slushy snow stings my face. I feel my feet slipping and grab at the nearest lamp post. My quarry stumbles to an ungainly halt. My chance. He teeters. A tram clangs and rattles by, a carriage in its wake. I catch the horse's musky animal scent. My quarry intends to run between the two vehicles and vanish into the snow-splintered melee of traffic and people.

I push myself from the lamp post and career through the homewards-hurrying crowds. He is about to take his step. The horse and carriage are perilously close. I lunge for him and my hand closes about his coat collar. We collide. The ground slithers from under my feet and then slams into my left arm. The man crashes on top of me. He swears and grunts but I hold on and roll over onto him.

Panting, aching and bruised, I grab his throat and squeeze.

"Stop struggling," I shout into his face. "I only want to ask you some questions."

His struggles cease. He drops his head back to the pavement as if resigned. "I've done nothing wrong."

"So why did you run?"

"You people are always hounding me."

"And why would that be? Shall we talk here or at the gendarme headquarters?"

"For the love of God, I can't talk here. We're drawing too much attention and, no, I don't want to go home to tea with you at your bloody headquarters either." His defiance returns. "What do you want to talk to me about anyway, as if I didn't know?"

"What do you think?"

Another sigh. "Dolf."

Four

I buy us both Turkish coffee and a pastry in a quiet, out-of-the way cafe. He is shaking. We are both cold and wet from our roll in the snow. My arm aches abominably, but I try to ignore it. There are few people in here. Most of Vienna is trying to get home. The snow is heavy now.

The café is warm and snug. I wait for Fritz to calm down. He seems nervous and constantly glances towards the door.

"Well? What can you tell about Dolf?" I ask.

"Someone…" He sighs, shakes his head. "Someone wants him dead."

"Yes, yes. I have already come to that conclusion. He is, after all, in hospital with a bullet wound."

"I know, but it's my fault."

I wait.

"I was offered money."

"Did *you* shoot him, Fritz?"

"Of course not. I couldn't do that. I know I'm occasionally in…well, in trouble, but I would never hurt anyone."

"So, why is this your fault?"

"I was offered money to keep certain people informed of Dolf's whereabouts. It was me who told them that he was going to the opera last night. I needed that money. I thought he'd crossed the wrong people and that they were out to teach him some sort of lesson. That would serve him right, as far as I was concerned, because me and him had fallen out. He accused me of embezzling him out of the earnings from his bloody paintings. I was offended and thought a few bruises and a black eye might bring him to his senses. I didn't know they were going to try to kill him, poor bastard."

"And did you? Embezzle him, I mean."

"No…well, business is business. You can't blame a man for trying to make a little profit. It was my commission. I've been doing all the leg work. It's hard to find anyone interested in his daubs."

Another glance towards the café door. His nervousness is infectious. "Look, I swear didn't know they were going to…"

"*They?*"

A glance. A shake of the head.

I make as if to stand. "Very well, if not here, we'll talk at—"

"The fella who approached me, he was Serbian and said he was a member of The Black Hand and that I should keep my mouth shut or else… You know."

I study him closely for signs that he is lying. Not easy, because it is obvious to me that Fritz Walter is adept at the art. What I do see, in his trembling and restlessness, is a frightened man. He has talked readily thus far, which also makes me think that he is relieved to share his secret and his guilt. I decide to go along with this.

"The Black Hand?"

A nod.

Why in God's name would an organisation like that be interested in a nobody like Hitler? Yes, they are Serbian and Hitler makes no secret of his hatred of the Serbians, but The Black Hand were formed by a group of army officers to fight for their country's independence from the Hapsburg Empire, not to silence one irrelevant bigot in a city of a thousand Serbian-haters.

Unless…

"Why Dolf? What is he involved in?"

"Nothing, I swear. No one would want him, anyway. He talks too much. He could never take orders."

"Who was it that approached you? What was his name?"

"I…I don't know."

"Everyone has a name. Even a false one."

"I was never given a name. Just a man in a bierkeller then meetings in a back street, at night. He said that the Ghost had sent him. He seemed frightened. Each time I saw him he was more…"

"Yes?"

"More unhinged, terrified."

"And this Ghost?"

"I don't know anything about him, or it."

A nod. No further explanation.

"Would you recognise the man you met in the bierkeller?"

"Please, Herr Leutnant, I cannot. They will kill me—"

"So if I walk away from here, you will be safe? You, whom scores of people saw wrestled to the ground by a policeman then led away, you will be safe?"

The truth dawns. He shakes his head.

"We can protect you, Fritz." Something of an idle boast and he knows it. Nevertheless, as I get to my feet and head for the door, he follows.

Five

Light still shines from the small windows of the barracks-like Gendarmerie Headquarters. I am saluted by the guards as I lead Walter inside. Even though we are charged with keeping the civilian peace, the gendarmerie is still military in style. The grey uniforms, the salutes and the layers of rank reek of army, death and glory. We're hated because of it. Our wise and benevolent ruler has not quite grasped the idea that the police are here to uphold the law, not crush rebellion and other actions seen as unpatriotic or disloyal to our rotting empire. Decaying, it is, like a fish, from the head downwards. An observation I keep to myself.

The offices of the Special Detective Department are on the second floor, a long climb this evening because, suddenly, I am tired. I am also hungry and ill-at-ease. Walter is still behind me. When we enter the office, I tell him to sit at my desk. He does so, nervously.

The light in here is electrical and glows a dim and dismal mustard colour. It flickers and crackles and makes fizzing sounds. I smell burning, on occasion. The wires, which are secured ostentatiously to the walls and across the ceiling in ugly wooden bridge-like cleats, are prone to overheating.

I visit Sergeant Goldschmidt, a Gendarme veteran who, since being transferred to this department, has grown an elaborate moustache and contented belly. He is near retirement, a little stiff-limbed these days, but as amiable as ever. Goldschmidt is the keeper of our considerable archive of files. I'm surprised he is still here at this hour.

"Herr Leutnant," he says. He is playing solitaire.

"I'm sorry to interrupt your busy schedule, Sergeant, but could you see if we have any files on Adolphus Hitler, and also on known members of the Black Hand."

"The Black Hand?"

"Yes."

"For you, Herr Leutnant, I put aside all my important tasks and snap to it." He chuckles to himself, glances at Walter, then whistling some unnameable tune, sets off towards our archive room.

"Leutnant Graf?"

My heart sinks. It is Captain Brunner. He stands in the doorway to his office. "Who is this?" He nods towards Walter.

"Fritz Walter, sir. He is connected to the shooting of Adolphus Hitler."

Panicked, Walter is on his feet. "No, no, I'm not—"

"Sit."

He does as he is told. What choice does he have?

I notice that Brunner is frowning "Adolphus…?"

"My case, sir. The one you gave me when I returned to duty this morning." The easy, meaningless case of a nobody shot in the street for no apparent reason and of no particular urgency or note.

"Oh, yes. The Heidler case. You asked Goldschmidt for The Black Hand files. Do you really think that the Serbians are behind this?"

I glance at Walter. He swallows heavily then nods. He is pale and trembling and looks as if he wants to run for the door. He has been in police offices before. It's easy to tell.

In turn, Brunner studies me.

"It seems so," I say.

"Mmmm," There is scepticism in his voice. His demeanour brightens into what looks like forced concern. "How are you, Leutnant?"

"Well, sir." A lie. I am tired. I am nervous. I would like a drink. I would like several drinks.

"Good. Good." He sees through me. "Examine your witness then go home. That's an order. We already have a Black Hand nest in Fleischmarkt under scrutiny. If they really are behind all this, then we will take the burden from your shoulders."

His office door closes. He is still watching, however. I can feel his curiosity and sense his nervousness at having me back in the fold. A moment, then Goldschmidt appears clutching a thick file. He lays it on my near empty desk. He produces another one and lays it on top of the first one. Then he grins at Walter.

"Your fame precedes you, Herr Hannisch."

I stare at Fritz Walter-who-isn't-Fritz Walter. He smiles ruefully and shrugs.

"Sir, meet Reinhold Hannisch, from the Sudetenland," Goldschmidt says good naturedly. "A mischief-maker with a penchant for petty crime."

Mischief-maker or not, he is certain when, after half an hour or so, he stabs his forefinger at one of the images Goldschmidt has brought in. It is a standard, poor-quality gendarme arrest portrait of a hard-faced, somewhat gaunt-looking character named Milomir Nikolic. He glares at us from the page.

He was arrested two years ago on suspicion of a robbery in which a bank clerk was beaten almost to death. No witnesses would come forward and he never even went to trial. Well, at least we now know that Walter, Hannisch, or whoever he might be, is telling the truth about the Black Hand's involvement.

"You promised to protect me," Hannisch says. He is frightened now. Seeing Nikolic's face has unnerved him.

"Yes, I did. You can sleep in a cell tonight."

"A cell? You bastard—"

"This isn't a hotel. And don't you think you deserve some punishment for betraying your friend to someone like Nikolic?" I stand. "Besides, what could be safer?"

"And tomorrow night?"

"We'll have Nikolic and his cronies in custody by then and you'll be free to go and beg Dolf's forgiveness."

"No. I won't be doing that."

"Why not? I thought he was your friend."

He grabs my arm, suddenly wild-eyed. "Leutnant," he says. "Be careful. There are times when I feel as if I am going mad. I have nightmares, and sometimes, waking dreams of war, of destruction."

"Guilt."

"Perhaps, because *he* is always at the heart of it."

"He? Nikolic?" His fervour makes me uneasy. "What are you talking about?"

"No, Dolf, surrounded by fire and suffering. I don't understand how or why. It is as if the walls of time have been fractured, and something is coming through. Keep away from him."

Six

Brunner invites me into his office on my second knock and waves towards the chair that faces him across his gleaming, heavy desk. He looks tired, but relaxed. He is smoking. The Captain is a veteran of the army, and a war or two. I imagine he once relished the blood and thunder of battle but is happy now for it to be a memory, and a source of drinking stories.

"Sit, sit, Jonas. Cigarette?"

I accept. He holds the flame of his ornate lighter to the cigarette's tip. I draw a deep breath and thank him.

He gives me a long, hard stare. "You look pale."

"It's my first day back at work. I've grown lazy."

He offers me a rueful smile. "Since you have disobeyed my order to go home, I can only assume that you need something."

"Yes. I want to make an arrest." I place the picture of Nikolic on the dark-stained desk.

Brunner grunts then shakes his head. "Not possible. This Heidler character isn't important enough for us to make our move at this moment."

He is right, but something is driving me now. It is hard to describe. The unease I have felt since my encounter with Hitler has grown into a more general feeling of detachment from the world around me. Until my conversation with Walter-Hannisch, I had put that down to the strain of my return to the world of the living, but now I'm not so sure. I am troubled by a sense that these events are not as they are supposed to be. Of course, no act of violence is what is *supposed to be*. This, however, is different. It is as if I have been pushed onto a parallel road that takes me alongside, rather than through, the familiar pathways and by-ways of real life. It's as if I can now see the seam that joins my own world to the real one. It is a dark, jagged crack in the fabric of reality, glimpsed out of the corner of my eye, but never there when I turn my gaze upon it.

Nonsense. I am exhausted.

It really is my inner struggle, the battle to regain normality and shake off the horror of what I did on that street those four months ago.

I am drawn back from my musing by Brunner's voice. "…must take this slowly." His tone is kind. He and I have always worked well together. But now he is under pressure. His superiors think that I should have been pensioned-off. He is taking a risk with his own career by giving me this chance. "Heidler doesn't matter. Yes, he is a human being. He is entitled to justice, but in the great scheme, he is of little importance. We cannot allow this matter to hinder a much bigger and more significant investigation. Something is afoot, Jonas. The Serbians are planning some great act of terror."

"Sir, they tried to kill Hitler for a reason. They wouldn't risk so much for a *nobody*."

"Listen Jonas." Brunner leans forward, eyes holding my own. "I think that, perhaps, you seek atonement."

"No, I—"

"Atonement for killing a man. It's a terrible thing to look into a someone's eyes and take their life. I know, believe you me. I *know*. Slavko Dordevic was going to cut that woman's throat. He was desperate and afraid. He had already taken a life…" A homemade bomb hurled into a bierkeller frequented by some herd of hulking, foreigner-hating patriots "…He was half-mad with guilt and fear. He was no longer a human being. You did a good thing, Jonas. You do not have to atone. We will bring Heidler, Hitler, whatever his damned name is, in for questioning as soon as he is well enough. We'll post guards in the hospital. This is too big for you to deal with alone. Do you understand? Go. Home. Finish your inquiries tomorrow, write a report then I will reassign you to something more interesting and worthy of your talents."

Seven

Home.

My second-floor apartment, once *our* apartment, is in the 5th District, the Margaretengürtel. It's a pleasant enough part of the city. I have a balcony which overlooks the street. We used to sit out there on hot summer evenings. We would smoke or drink wine, or simply talk and watch the world slip by.

It is still as you left it, Adela. No electricity. The soft, plump armchairs arranged about the small fireplace, which has been laid for a fire by the maid, Sara. Remember her, Adela? She is to be married herself soon. She looks after me well, but I can tell she misses you almost as much as I do. She is always pleasant and polite to me, but it is skin-deep. She is a little afraid of me now. She blames me for your departure. She is right, of course. It is my fault. Or is it Slavko's fault, the man with the knife who threatened the woman with the baby, the man who was slain for his sin by a police detective with a gun?

The photograph taken to mark our engagement is still on the mantlepiece with all the other ornaments you left behind. It is a little faded now. There we are, two serious, slightly frightened-looking people staring rigidly from a background that is obviously a fake, but beautiful, garden. You are seated on a wicker chair. I stand behind you, hand on your small, delicate shoulder. I can still feel its roundness, the way it fits into my palm, and the roughly textured lace and soft silk of your elaborate blouse.

It was in the restaurant of the Hotel Josefshof am Rathaus where I first saw you, Adela. I was with my fiancé, bored as we made polite small talk and picked at our veal. You caught my eye, seated a few tables away, looking as bored as I felt. Opposite you was a young man in expensive-looking clothes and blessed with immaculate hair and a moustache he did not look old enough to have cultivated. He chattered on and on at you. You nodded politely but your attention strayed and you gazed vacantly about the room. Your companion seemed as unaware of your disinterest as dear sweet, but dull, Irene was of mine.

Our stares met.

Our stares held.

You had fine features, delicate and yet I could already see strength of your will. I could see intelligence and fire. Your gaze lingered long enough to discomfort me. Then moved on and left me oddly bereft.

Unable to sit still a moment longer, I excused myself from my betrothed and wandered out of the restaurant and across the hotel's foyer to its entrance, where I lit a cigarette and watched the comings and goings on the street outside.

Surely, I could not go through with the marriage. Irene was a beautiful young woman, her family wealthy with powerful connections and already perturbed that their daughter was on the cusp of marrying a lowly police detective. But I felt nothing that resembled love, not that I was an expert, but surely, she should be more than a sister to me.

That was when I became aware of a presence beside me. A woman. Sure it was Irene, I turned and was startled –

no, that is too weak a word, shocked perhaps – to see that it was you, Adela.

"May I have a cigarette?" you said.

I obliged you. You drew in the smoke, eyes half closed and obviously an expert in the art. You were also refreshingly uncaring of the disapproving glares you received from passers-by.

"Are you having as delightful time as I am?" you said. There was mischief in your sparkling grey eyes.

"I think so."

"My mother and father thought it would be a great thing to throw me together with young Mr Donner. My God, he is dull."

So was Irene, but I could not bring myself to say so. It seemed unkind, but what I did next was even more cruel than an un-heard insult. "Would you like to go for a walk?" I said.

You looked at me, startled, but also amused. That smile. Oh God, how it brought light into your face. Then mischief. "I would be honoured."

We made no excuses. I paid for mine and Irene's meal at the reception desk and asked for a motor taxi to be called to take her home. We then gathered my coat and hat and your cape and we left the hotel together. We walked arm in arm for a while, and I think I was in love with you by the time we reached the end of the first street. I hailed a fiacre, told the driver to take us around the heart of the city, and kissed you as we sat in its open carriage. Ah, the taste of you, the scent of you, the heat and sweetness.

I swear I can smell your perfume now. A claim made by many whose loved one is dead. But you're still alive, aren't you Adela. No one will tell me where you ran to, because they are afraid of what I might do to you. Love conquers all, or so they say. Well, it's a lie. It could not conquer my drinking and night terrors, or the daytime terrors I inflicted on *you*, Adela, because I cannot rid myself of that moment. That moment when I saved a life by taking one.

Plead with you to return to me, that's what I will do. I will throw myself unashamedly at your feet, weep and beg forgiveness and make promises no man can ever keep. I would never raise a hand to you. I never did, even at my lowest. But you still came to fear me, and a woman should never be afraid of her husband.

I crouch before the hearth, light the fire and watch the flame devour the paper and kindling. There is a reassuring smell of smoke. I stay where I am until the fire has taken hold enough for me to feed it with coal. The pungent smoke-odour changes. I smell another unpleasant stink.

Burning clothes, hair, flesh, as if the grate is piled hight with emaciated, near-skeletal corpses.

I recoil and struggle to my feet. Imagination only. Nothing else. Not real.

Yet so very real.

I hurry across to the cabinet from which I retrieve a vodka bottle and glass. My hand shakes. The bottle clinks against the rim of the tumbler. I drink. I pour again then make my way back to my chair and sit once more.

Silence is the enemy here. It is a solid weight. It is pure emptiness. It feels as if I only exist when I am at my work. This day has been a relief from the endless weeks I spent here, slowly driving my wife away until I was truly alone and the silence that had been boiling at the edges of my life finally poured in to drown me.

Drink. That was, and is, my salvation. The wreckage to which I cling. Tired, I close my eyes, wishing for the blessed oblivion of sleep.

That perfume again, stronger this time, sweet and clear.

My eyes open and there she is, perched on the armchair opposite: demure, elegant. I can't see her eyes in the shadows but I can feel the intensity of her gaze and the mischief that lies behind her carefully sculptured façade of respectability.

"Adela…"

I struggle to my feet and lurch towards her. She looks up, smiles and dissolves into restless shadow and the flicker of firelight. I collapse to my knees, my forehead on the chair on which the phantom had been sitting. I sob. A broken, degraded wreck of a human being, no longer a man, but a weeping child.

Disgusted, I haul myself back upright then return to my own chair and the half empty bottle. I drink. Silence falls.

The Devil comes to me in that silence. He shows me over and over again that Hell is the flash of a revolver and the sharp explosive concussion of a fired bullet.

It is the recoil.

It is Slavko's head, snapped back as it fractures and breaks and loses any semblance of humanity.

I swallow the remains of my drink and reach for the bottle, now on the floor beside me. The Devil chuckles from the seething mass of shadow that forms in the corners of the room and in the blackness behind Adela's chair. He sounds pleased with his handiwork. Delighted with his new disciple.

Does he haunt Brunner, who marched to war and killed countless other human beings yet seems unaffected? Does the Devil visit him to reminisce?

I stare across at the darkness and I can see the Devil now. Oh yes, there he is. A man who stands arrogantly upright with one hand jammed into his jacket pocket. His eyes are hard and cold. They are alive with white-hot fire, and yet, behind them lies a soulless, howling void.

I've seen those eyes before.

Adolphus Hitler. The Devil wears his skin.

Eight

In the morning, I walk to the to the Südbahnhof railway station, where, according to the clientele at the Meldemannstrasse Men's Dormitory, Hitler sometime earns a wage shovelling snow. I doubt that I will learn much more there than I know already, or come any closer to the reason why The Black Hand should want Hitler dead, but there is always a chance that a little light might be shed on the mystery, and I need to be satisfied that I have explored every avenue in my inquiries.

Brunner would probably tell me I am wasting my time, which is why I make for the station before reporting in at the Gendarmerie Headquarters. He wants me to step away from the investigation, but I cannot tolerate loose ends, a case not resolved.

At least, that is what I tell myself.

It has snowed all night, folding Vienna in a soft magical coating of ermine. The air is clean and bitterly cold; a dry, solid cold that refreshes and stimulates rather than discomforts. This is a beautiful city, but that beauty hides the slow deterioration of its Empire. It is a mask that covers the lined, decaying face of a corrupt, dying old man. Oh, there is glamour aplenty, but it is an illusion. While the rest of the world gropes its way into this new century, our empire and its rulers hold us back with all their might.

The station itself is as magnificent as a palace. The vast frontage resembles a Greek temple. The main structures extend off into the distance, the facade broken by a regimented parade of huge arched windows. The roads around its entrance are clogged with carriages and more motor cars that I have ever seen in any one place at one time.

The sky is still darkening towards iron grey, The snow makes walking perilous. Indeed, a lady swathed in a luxurious fur almost falls in front of me. Fortunately, her companion manages to hold onto her. His hat is knocked from his head. They both laugh. Her dignity remains intact. I feel a pang of jealousy.

I draw my identification from my coat as I pass through the entrance, ready to brandish it to remove any obstruction. I have no patience. My head once more feels as if it is fracturing under the hammer blows of a hangover. My mouth is dry and there is a foul taste there.

Once inside the grand, echoing edifice, I look for anyone who might be a railway official. I make my way to the platform, where a train awaits. Steam billows from between its wheels and spills from its smokestack. Through the hot, dirty fog I see the silhouette of a man bent over a shovel as he scrapes at the platform. It's as good a place as any to begin my inquiries. He pauses in his work as I emerge from the swirl of warm mist, smiles at my greeting and frowns at the sight of my identification.

"Can you direct me to your supervisor?" I say.

The man, a wizened, craggy specimen with a good-hearted twinkle in his eye, takes a drag on his cigarette. "You'll need Wenzel Aignor, he's in charge of keeping the platforms clean and tidy. Bit of a martinet. Why do you want him?"

I am about to politely inform him that it is none of his business, then stop myself. "Actually, you might be able to help me. I'm making inquiries about a gentleman who works here on occasion, doing what you're doing, in fact."

"Who might that be, Herr Leutnant?"

"Adolphus Hitler."

The man chuckles ruefully. "Dolf? That miserable little bastard? Yes, I know him well enough."

"What's he like?" The man has already answered part of my question, but I need to hear it. I need to hear that he is a mere mortal man and not some demonic creature unleashed on the world to bring about its destruction.

"Angry." The man shakes his head and chuckles ruefully. "He never stops being angry. We've all had the sharp edge of his tongue. Usually when we dare to disagree with some rambling political point he's trying to make. Not that I talk politics very often. There's no minister of state who's ever done anything to make my life any better. And yes, I know you're an officer of the law and I need to keep my mouth shut, but I'm too old and tired to care about that."

"Don't worry. I'm not about to arrest anyone for holding an opinion."

The man's wry smile turns to scepticism. "I find that hard to believe, Herr Leutnant."

"Would you say that he's…" I look for an appropriate word but give up. "Mad?"

"Sometimes, definitely. It comes and goes with him. Works hard though. Can't fault him on that."

"Do you know if he is affiliated with any political groups?"

"I take that to mean something shady. You think he's a revolutionary or an anarchist?"

"You tell me."

"A good detective's answer." The man takes a last drag at the tiny stub of his cigarette and drops into the slush. "I don't think he is, because none of them anarchist gangs would have him. Why are you asking about him anyway?"

"Sometime tried to kill him."

"Really? Bloody hell. Why was that? An argument? Someone trying to stop him talking about the bloody opera?" Another chuckle. "Sorry, that wasn't funny. Is he badly injured?"

"He'll survive. And no, we don't think it was during an argument. It looks as if it was an assassination attempt. Have you any ideas who might want to do that?"

I know, of course, but I have no motive. I have strands but no pattern.

"Not off-hand."

Time to leave. There's nothing new to learn here.

The man has other ideas. "I tell you this…" He glances left and right, as if looking for eavesdroppers. "Lately…Well, I don't like him being near me. I mean, he isn't anyone's friend, but something is wrong with…with everything, when he's around. It makes my skin crawl. I can't explain it, but there are times when I could believe that the bastard is not quite human." He chuckles ruefully. "Don't listen to me. I'm a foolish old man who spends too much time in the bierkeller and not enough at home with his wife. She's always warning me that beer will addle my brain one day. She's right. Women are always right, eh, Herr Leutnant?"

It takes a moment for me to understand what he is saying. "Mmm, yes, yes, they are. Thank you for your help." I yearn for Adela to tell me that I am wrong about something, anything. To be angry with me, then forgiving, then tender, then cold. That is the way between a man and a woman, a constant struggle to find the light of happiness, the joyous reunion after some trivial argument or sentence of silence. I miss it. I want her.

I leave, in a hurry. Partly because I do not want to hear about Hitler being something other than human, but mostly because I feel the ache of loss and the sting of tears. I do not wish to weep in front of this gnarled old man who looks as if he hasn't shed a tear since childhood and would have little sympathy for any man who showed such weakness.

I had needed reassurance. Instead, I have been given more fuel to fire the madness simmering away in my own alcohol-addled mind.

...something is wrong with...with everything when he's around. It makes my skin crawl. I can't explain it, but there are times when I could believe that the bastard is not quite human...

Nine

"Good morning, Fritz, or is it Reinhart, or Johann or Hans?"

"Everyone calls me Fritz." Hennisch doesn't look as if a night in our cells has done him any harm. Indeed, he looks refreshed, as if from a good night's sleep. Here then, is a man who has seen the inside of a police cell before – on more than one occasion according to Sergeant Goldschmidt – and for whom it holds no terrors

"Fritz it is then."

"I wasn't expecting to see you again Herr Leutnant."

"Well, here I am, and about to buy you lunch. Afterwards, you will take me to the place where you met our friend Milomir Nikolic."

His happy-go-lucky expression dissolves into fear, "No, I'm sorry, but no. I can't. These are dangerous people—"

"Now, now, Fritz. Sergeant Goldschmidt has uncovered a wealth of information on your criminal activities. Petty crimes, perhaps – fraud, deception – but they won't help your case when you appear in court charged with being an accessory to an attempted murder, will they."

"Oh, come now. Surely threats like this are beneath you, Herr Leutnant." He is trying to be recover his cool-and-collected persona, but I can hear the tremor in his voice and see the terror in his eyes.

"Let's go," I say and take his arm. "I'm hungry." And still hung over from last night's self-pity and alcoholic indulgence.

It is snowing again. The cold is no longer clean and refreshing. This cold eats through coats, suits and shirts to burrow deep into the flesh beneath. My fingers are quickly numb despite my gloves. I can feel the weight of my revolver in its holster under my arm and wonder if I would be able to fire it if the need arose.

And not only because of my cold-stiffened fingers.

The buildings that border the street are dark against the white. The snow has a clean, pure feel to it, although on the road, the endless parade of carriages, carts and motor vehicles are turning it to a filthy mush.

We find a café. Inside it is gloriously warm. The tiled floor is wet with melted snow carried in on the customers' shoes and boots. I order coffees and pastries. Both Hennisch and I set to with the enthusiasm of hungry men.

"Once you have shown me what I want to see," I say, leaning back, satiated and warm now, "you're free to go."

"Are you sure about that Herr Leutnant?"

"I'm sure. Consider yourself lucky, considering the fact that you betrayed your friend—"

"Dolf has no friends."

"—I'm sure your treachery will haunt the sleepless hours. That will be punishment enough. Hitler might have died. He was meant to, and you would have played your part in his murder. As it is, well, it looks as if he will survive, so no harm done, eh?"

Hannisch grunts and covers his discomfort by lighting a cigarette.

"So, the least you can do for me is take me to the place where you earned your thirty pieces of silver."

"If it will help."

Who knows what will help. I am grasping at phantoms.

Back outside into the freezing snow under a steel grey sky. We barge through the oncoming crowds, a succession of human shapes, hunched, features pinched. The numbness spreads to my feet. The snow stings my face. The effects of the coffee and food quickly wear off.

"We will need to take a fiacre or a tram," Hannisch says. "The bierkeller's in Spittelberg."

A clutch of cobbled streets and old buildings between Siebensterngasse and Burggasse. In decline, the perfect haunt for someone like Hannisch.

"What were you doing there? Ah, of course, looking to pay for a little feminine company, no doubt."

"I don't need to pay for women. I was thirsty. I needed a drink."

The first transport we find is a fiacre, a horse drawn open carriage pulled by a miserable looking nag, and driven by a sullen figure half-hidden in a pile of blankets and blessed with a bright red nose. The paintwork on the vehicle looks as worn and battered as its driver. The man doesn't look happy when I tell him where we want to go.

"That's a long way," he mutters darkly. "Not much of a place to visit."

"A fare's a fare," I say.

I'm glad to slump into the carriage. I'm tired and still suffering from the after-effects of last night's alcoholic self-mutilation. I pay little attention to the journey but pull my coat about myself, a ratty blanket over my knees, and close my eyes. Snow feathers my face.

I remember again how that first evening with Adela had ended with the two of us huddled together in a fiacre, although it was in a much better state than this one. That moment had been deep, intense. It almost made me cry. Those few minutes, her body pressed close to mine, had been the bridge between desire and love. I had known then that I would marry this woman.

God, I want her back.

Spittelberg is not an inspiring place; cobbled streets, many of them narrow and shadowed, houses that look to be past their best. I pay the driver and watch the fiacre trundle away. The sight of its exit makes me so lonely, I'm even glad of Hannisch's company.

"All right, Fritz old friend," I say and almost mean it. "Where to now?"

He gives me an odd look then leads the way into a side street, which is home to unprepossessing establishment called the Werner Bierkeller. There are shutters across the windows. The door is firmly locked. It does not appear to be a particularly salubrious establishment. Nor would it be, if it tolerates the presence of Serbians within its hallowed walls. They are not often welcome in Vienna's better class watering holes.

Neither are men like Hannisch, come to that.

"It looks closed to me," I say.

"On the contrary, Herr Leutnant, the Werner is always open for business. You just need to be on their guest list."

"And how do you go about adding your name to such a list?"

"You have to be recommended."

"Ah, an exclusive establishment." I clap my hand on Hannisch's shoulder. "So, are you going to vouch for me?"

A rueful chuckle. "They will know you are a police officer the moment they see you."

"Get on with it. I haven't got all day."

Hannisch sighs, then crosses the alley and raps his knuckles on the door. A moment, then a shutter slides across. All I can see are a pair of bloodshot eyes.

"It's Fritz. I've brought a guest along with me."

The eyes flick in my direction. "No guests. Tell him to piss off."

Impatient and weary now, I produce my identification. "Open up, now, or I'll bring a few friends and an axe back with me. I'm sure we'll find plenty to entertain us in your establishment. Or," I move in close, "we can keep it between us."

The shutter slams back into place. I hear the rattle of locks, then the door opens, and we are hurriedly ushered inside. There is silence. The customers sit at shadow-darkened tables that creak under the weight of beer jugs and tankards. A waiter in a stained apron seems frozen halfway from the bar to a table, yet another jug in his large hand. The air is heavy with cigarette and pipe smoke. Every person in the room stares at us, and it feels as if every one of them wants to beat us to a pulp.

There are women here. They are provocatively dressed, with more flesh on view than would be considered decent in even the most liberal hostelry.

The ones I can see clearly through the fug do not appear to be in the best of health.

Mein Host bars our path. He is a brute of a man, built more for the boxing ring than the care of his customers.

"Well?" he growls.

"I need to speak with a patron of yours, a Milomir Nikolic."

"A fucking Serbian?"

"I wouldn't know."

"Why'd you bring him here?" Mein Host jabs his enormous finger in my face but directs his question at Hannisch, who shrinks back, obviously scared. I feel the tension winding tighter. I don't think my badge will protect me here.

"I didn't have a choice…I…"

"I don't want to see you back here, you understand me, Fritz?"

"Now, now." I squeeze between the two men. "No need for bad feeling. I don't want to know what goes on in here. I just want to talk to Nikolic. I know he comes here because that's where he and my friend Fritz first met with each other. Unless you're lying Fritz…"

"No, definitely not lying Herr Leutnant."

Movement, glimpsed, sensed. Movement in a room where no one moved. Someone taking advantage of the gloom, a shadow among shadows.

"Hey, you—"

The man explodes into motion, no longer attempting to hide his escape. I make to pursue him but find my way blocked by a handful of large, angry-looking characters. Desperation makes me reckless, and I wrench my revolver from its holster under my arm.

"Out of my way."

The men stumble back. My quarry freezes, half turned towards me. His arm is extended in my direction. The gesture puzzles me. Then I understand and dive for the filthy, beer-sodden dirt floor just as he fires.

The bierkeller erupts into a hell of shouting, screaming and stumbling, struggling, fear-driven bodies. I don't know if anyone has been hit. There is no time to find out. I force my way through the tangle and panic in time to see the gunman wrench open a door at the far end of the room. I follow and find myself climbing a narrow set of stone steps.

The man is already at the top. He turns to glare at me. His eyes are wide. He looks mad, insane almost. He raises the weapon once more.

"No, Milomir Nikolic, stop. I only want to talk."

Another shot. I duck sideways, press myself against the wall. I feel the shockwave of the bullet.

A door slams open. Harsh light and cold air. Street sounds, the clop of hooves, rattle of wheels, shouts, laughter, the donkey-bray of a motor car horn.

Exhausted already, I ascend the remaining steps and emerge onto the corner of a busy street. There is little glamour here. The houses are crooked, and in need of repair. The snow has been churned to slush. I look for my quarry. No sign. Too many people, too much traffic.

No.

There.

Running across the road, arm raised.

I follow. A horse rears, its driver swears. A motor car skids, its horn blares. I don't care. I must keep Nikolic in sight. If I cannot catch him, I will follow him.

A large, cumbersome motor taxi trundles to a halt. Nikolic talks to the driver who sits, cold and morose, in the open front seat. An urgent request. Money changes hands. Then Nikolic opens the door to climb inside. I force myself into a fast run. My chest and throat burn from effort and from the cold air I am forcing into my lungs.

The engine revs. The driver reaches out to release the brake lever. The car lurches forward, slowed by a horse and cart that cuts in front of it, and by the slippery conditions.

My chance.

I lunge at the door handle, but it slips from my grasp. I grab at the spare wheel clamped to the back of the vehicle. I hold on, run then leap onto the back and cling to the wheel. My feet rest on the rear bumper. I crouch so that Nikolic doesn't see me through the rear window. It is a precarious perch, but fortunately the motor taxi cannot pick up much speed in these conditions.

My arms quickly ache, my legs are cramped, and my hands are freezing and stiff, but I will hold on. By God, I will hold on.

Ten

Neither the gunman nor the driver seem aware that I am clinging to the back of the cab. Others will see me, and I pray to the deity I have ignored for most of my life that they will not alert the driver.

The journey is a trip through a frozen Hell. A brutal, icy wind tears at my clothes and my hair. My hat is long gone. My eyes stream with tears and my lungs burn from the bitter coldness of the air. But I hang on. I will not let go. *I will not let go.*

Time loses its meaning.

The world is cramped muscles. The bone-crushing jolts of the cab.

And the cold.

Oh God, the cold.

It tears through me. It burns my face and stiffens my muscles. It numbs my hands and feet, and freezes them in place. This is an act of sheer insanity. This is obsession, not policing. I cannot release this case from my grasp any more than I can let go of the spare wheel, to which it feels as if I am frozen.

I close my eyes and hang on and try to blank out the pain and the strain. I try to step outside the moment.

Then, thankfully, the cab slows. I wait until it is almost stopped then release my hold and attempt to land on my feet, but there is still enough momentum to throw me backwards and once more to the ground.

I lay in the slush, dampness added to the misery of my journey. I roll over and struggle to my feet. We are in a busy street in what I recognise as the Fleischmarkt. If anyone saw my ungainly leap from the cab, they keep it to themselves. No one pays me any attention. I get to my feet as quickly as I can and find a hiding place in the doorway to a large, ancient-looking house. There is plenty of shadow here, and Nikolic will not be looking for me.

The cab has come to a halt, perhaps ten metres further on. I leave my refuge and set off towards it, losing myself in the irregular stream of people hurrying along the pavement. I am out of breath and shivering violently. I will be lucky not succumb to, at best, a cold or, more probably, pneumonia.

Nikolic emerges for the taxi, pays the driver, then glances back up the street. The gesture is furtive, nervous.

Again, that desperate, frightened look. His eyes are wide and there is little sanity in his gaze. I swear that he is talking to himself. He shakes his head, bats at some unseen annoyance then sets off at a brisk walk along the pavement. I follow, from as discreet a distance as I can manage. I am bruised and my clothes are soaking wet. The dampness is turning to cold. The daylight is fading, early, although the iron sky had never allowed much sunlight through anyway.

As always, Vienna is busy. Clattering carriages and sputtering automobiles, trams and people. The city is magical despite the sleet. The buildings twinkle with newly ignited light. They loom over me as I pass by, vast and majestic, and even as I leave the centre and the houses grow more modest and poorer and the clothes of the people I meet become less grand, there is still a smell, a sound, a tightness of the air, an electric tingle that is Vienna.

My quarry turns suddenly into the mouth of a dark, narrow alley. I wait a few moments then follow.

Tenement houses and apartments line the alleyway like cliff faces. There is no light here, other than the uncertain glow of illumination that leaks in from the main street. There are no people that I can see. Nikolic makes for a faceless, three-storey ugliness that acts as the far wall of a cul-de-sac. Light shines, shifting and uncertain, from only one window, up on the third floor. There is no electricity here, only oil lamps and candles.

I do not like that house.

And that light, it is a flickering silvery illuminance that spills over to briefly paint the wall below and occasionally flares bright enough to stain the cobbles and the walls of the neighbouring tenements. It is unnatural, unwholesome. Somehow it pervades the whole building.

I break from the shadows as Nikolic arrives at the building's front door and fumbles in his coat pockets, presumably for a key.

"Milomir. Wait."

He looks round, wildly, seeking the source of the voice. He sees me. I push my hand into my coat and grasp the handle of my revolver. Nikolic doesn't bring out his own weapon, however. He shrinks back. I keep my hand on my gun. I don't want to use it and pray that the man who now cowers at my approach won't force me to shoot.

I raise my free hand, trying to placate him.

"I only wish to talk. I want to know about the Ghost."

"No, no, no. Go away. Leave this place as fast as you can. The wall of time is broken. The walls of the world are tumbling down…"

"What do you mean. What are the walls of time? Tell me, please. I need to know."

"No. No."

"Why did you try to kill Adolphus Hitler? Surely, he's nothing to you."

"He has to die…"

"Why, Milomir, tell me why."

"The Ghost… The Ghost desires it."

"Who is this Ghost? Milomir, I want to help you." Do I? No, of course I don't, and yet I feel sympathy for this shivering frightened, barely sane wreck before me.

He mutters something and once again bats at an imaginary assailant.

"…have to stop it. Have to stop the Ghost."

Then he does wrench his gun from his pocket.

I shout at him to stop, but he fires.

The bullet goes wild. I dodge to my left. Instinct.

He wrenches the door open. Another door. It feels suddenly as if I am pursuing him through some crazed building, chasing him from one room to the next, each one more bizarre than the other.

I run, revolver in hand now. I shout for him to stop and to wait.

The door is slammed shut in my face. I fall against it, hands splayed on the rough, battered wood. And I feel it then. My fingers sink into the door as if the wood has turned to mush. The building vibrates. It twists and distorts. The walls stretch and shrink as if breathing. There is something in there, something I cannot understand or imagine.

I hear voices. A man yells and rants, there is fire and noise.

I can't stand it anymore and push myself back.

I stare at the house. It is ugly. Plain. That odd, disturbing silver light shifts uncertainly in its window.

The wall of time is crumbling…

"Do not move."

The voice has authority I recognise.

I don't want to obey. I want to watch the light. It holds the answer. It is hard to tear my gaze from it.

"Throw down your weapon and raise your hands. Now, quickly, or we fire."

I hear their boots crunch through the slush.

"I am a police officer," I shout back. "Leutnant Graf."

"Shut up and stand still. Raise your hands or I will shoot."

Then there are dark shapes. One of them holds a revolver.

"For God's sake, I am Leutnant Jonas Graf from the Special Detective Department of the Vienna Gendarmerie."

"Oh Christ," the armed assailant groans. "Graf? What in the devil's name are you doing here?"

Leutnant Reiter. Not my best friend in the Department, and the last person I want to see at that moment.

"It seems our investigations have collided." I keep my voice steady, but I am trembling, and not only from the cold. "May I lower my hands, Reiter?"

"Yes, yes, of course." He sounds angry and frustrated. "What investigation? Why would it bring you here? To hell with you, Graf. Months of work. Bloody months, fucking ruined you bastard." He waves towards the house. "Do you think they'll stay here now? They've probably scuttled off already, the moment they heard me shout 'police'."

"They're still there." I am as startled as Reiter by my own certainty. "And you must raid the house."

He steps back, shakes his head and seems suddenly frightened, which is unlike him. Reiter is a big, broad brute of a man, the first to wade into a fight, seemingly afraid of no one. "No, no, our orders are to watch."

The two other detectives who stand at his shoulders have that same haunted look about them. I recognise it as the one worn by Nikolic.

"They know we're out here, you fool. Look at us, standing in the middle of the lane, in full view," I shout and wonder why I am so angry and upset by this. "There is no point in watching anymore. Something is wrong with that house. We have to get inside Something…something bad is happening inside its walls."

The walls of time.

Broken.

Reiter is back on me. His face is a few centimetres from my own. The desperation in his anger matches mine. He is afraid to enter that building. I understand his fear, because I feel it too. Whatever has infected Nikolic has found its way into Reiter's head, and those of his two henchmen. I'm beginning to wonder if it has infected me as well. "Go away, Graf. Bugger off, now, or I will report you to Brunner for incompetence."

Now that is a threat I cannot shrug off. I am already skating on the thinnest of ice as far as the good captain is concerned. I am supposed to have called my investigation to a halt.

I walk away. It is hard because the house is calling to me. It begs me to turn about, pound on its door and demand entrance. My last sight of Reiter and his men is of them standing in the street, staring at the building, faces made bright and stark, then shadowed and invisible by the flicker of the silver light from that third-floor window.

Eleven

I go home. My clothes are soaked through. I am cold and shiver uncontrollably. I feel unwell, and a freezing ride through the streets in the open carriage of a fiacre doesn't help, despite the blanket thoughtfully provided by the driver. Mounting the stairs to my apartment is like climbing a mountain. I am light-headed and feverish.

I manage to light a fire, then, after washing as best I can in bowl of cold water because I cannot be bothered to heat any, put on my bed clothes and dressing gown. It is too early to go to bed, and I won't sleep anyway without help from the bottle I have taken from its shelf, and which I now use to fill the first tumbler of the evening. I should eat, but I have no appetite.

The bottle's neck clinks against the rim of the glass. I try to understand what has gone wrong. Until I followed Milomir Nikolic into that grubby little alleyway in the Fleishmarket, I was a tough, professional detective. Damaged, yes, fractured and troubled, but when it came to my work, still up to scratch.

But now.

I am nervous, but unsure why.

I am afraid, but uncertain as to exactly what I am afraid of.

I am haunted by the house, that old, mouldering tenement that is like so many other buildings in the poorer corners of the city. It is, at once, no different, but also very different. I find myself transfixed by the memory of the unearthly silver light flickering from that third-floor window. I recall the way that the door and the walls gave under my touch, as if made of flesh.

Imagination, of course, but that whole, dingy little side street felt wrong, as if it has been infected by whatever is in the house. Something awful emanates from those bricks or, more likely, from whatever rotten heart beats within its walls.

No, no. Nonsense. It is a house. A building. It is mortar, wood and glass. Nothing more.

Is this unease because the house is a hideout for members of the Black Hand? Perhaps I have lost my nerve and am no longer able to take the fight to a vicious gang of anarchists. No, Nikolic seemed as scared as I was. He had gone into the house only because he was compelled to do so, not because he wanted to.

And my old foe, Leutnant Reiter, the Bull, the Brute, promoted because of his willingness to break bones in order to protect the Empire. He had been too afraid to raid the place. Normally, he would have not held back, but this time, he had been frightened, unable to act, unable to leave.

I drain my schnapps and pour another.

It burns its way down.

I stare into the fire, determined to drink myself into unconsciousness, here, in my ancient armchair. First I will grow maudlin and weep over Adela. Another glass and I can smell her perfume. I can hear the rustle of her skirts and feel the softness of her clothing and of her lips. I can taste her.

I whisper her name and am sure she is here.

I close my eyes and feel her touch, a gentle trail of fingertips over my face. When I open them again, I see her, crouched before me, that mischievous smile on her lips. This cannot be. Has she returned to me?

"Adela?"

She places her hands on my thighs and rises so that we can kiss. Her breath is hot, her lips soft. I draw her to me and feel the slight roughness of her lace blouse, hear the rustle of her skirts. Her perfume, her presence, overwhelm me. I slide from the chair and lower her to the floor. She is light and shade. She is a chimera and yet every touch, every kiss is real and explodes on my flesh. There are bursts of white-hot light in my soul. This is madness. My mind has finally broken, but I don't care. Adela is here. I lose myself in her skirts, I feel the softness of her thighs. I feel her heat and scrabble at my own clothes so that I can sink into the insanity fully and find joy.

Together now. Joined. One. Waves of delight shudder through me. Adela sighs and moans. I kiss her face, her throat.

Her lips are to my ear, her breath a sighing wind. "The walls of time are fractured," she whispers. "The real is being twisted until it breaks—"

I want her to stop. To shut up. I don't want to hear this. I twist my head to kiss her again. And there is nothing. My palms are pressed against the rug. I am on my hands and knees. My glass is on its side, contents spilled. The only heat is from the fireplace where logs crackle and flames dance. I am not alone. I look up and there he is.

The Devil.

He threads his way through the shadows that dance in the corners of the room. He boils from the flames in the grate and gathers flesh about his rotten, dark soul. He sculpts the landscapes of his face until he is human and wearing the skin of the man who is the core of this nightmare.

He doesn't move. He doesn't flinch. He isn't aware of me. He is constructed from the dance of fire and shadow that paints the very air in here. But I see him. I know him. Those empty eyes glare from deep in their sockets, windows to a howling void where there should be a soul.

Then he begins to shout. His incoherent ranting suddenly fills the apartment. He brings his fist down onto his other palm, a brutish drumbeat that accompanies each hateful syllable. Spittle flies from his mouth.

The glow of the fire paints the side of his face in shifting orange light. I smell the stink of burning flesh. I see figures dance in the flames and in the maddened light. I see rank upon rank of silhouettes march across the wall behind him. A crowd roars from every shadow-stained corner. "Hail Victory! Hail Victory!" they chant. "Sieg Heil! Sieg Heil!" Then the rage of their voices is the scream of some air machine that dives, howling and wailing from the sky above my roof then shatters into the whistle of a bombshell and the hell-roar of an explosion. I am pummelled to my knees by the din, by the endless storm of Hitler's tirade, by the apocalyptic thunder of battle and the screams of the dying and there is madness in the orange light and in the dark. It must stop.

It. Must. Stop.

I clamp my hands over my ears.

I howl for it to end.

And there is silence.

But for the crackle of the fire and the hard rhythm of my breath.

I struggle once more back into my chair. I reach for the bottle.

And remember Nikolic's wild tirade and Adela's soft whisper.

It is as if the walls of time are fractured, and something is coming through…

Twelve

The fire is out when I wake. The light is grey. The air in the room is cold. I have slept in the armchair. I am stiff, and my skull aches. I was shown something. The air machines. The vast land-leviathans. The hell of smoke and fire.

Where did they come from? My own mind? Impossible. Those visions were of things I could never have conceived. They were too vivid. It was as if that crack in the world, which still haunts and tantalises me as soon as I open my eyes, yawned a little wider to reveal...what? The future? My own encroaching madness? Some alien world that lies on the other side of the thin wall that contains our Earth?

I need to act in some way.

I must return to the hospital, face the Devil and assure myself that he is a mere mortal man who can do me no harm whatsoever and that my dream, hallucination, whatever it was, came from my own mind. That the real had not been twisted.

To do that, I must confront the monster.

My identification has turned away any protest or question, even from the two gendarmes who sleepily guard the ward entrance. I hear the usual coughing. I smell the usual human stenches. Someone calls for help. His endlessly repeated pleas go unheard. There is a mindlessness behind them. It is as if he needs to hear his own voice to prove his existence.

I make to remove my hat, out of habit, and remember that I lost it during my mad carriage ride. I run my hand through my unbrushed hair then enter the ward. I make for his bed. I can see him, sat up. Not reading, not eating, simply staring.

"How are you Adolphus?"

"What do you want? Have you found them? The people who did this to me, have you found them?"

"Perhaps."

"Perhaps? Is that all you have to say? And who are these *perhaps* murderers? Jews? Serbians?"

"Who are *you*?" I say.

He looks momentarily puzzled then smiles a chilly, non-smile. "I am not yet who I can be."

"What do you mean by that?"

"There is something for me to do, a task for me to complete. I have been certain of it since this…" He waves a hand across his bandaged wound.

"What is this task?"

He shakes his head. "I'm not sure. But it waits for me."

"Who told you?"

He glares at me and I see the howling waste wilderness again. "No one."

I hold his stare this time. I search the abyss. I am looking for a clue, but there is nothing. He is flesh formed about a hollow well of darkness.

"I just know," he says.

I can't bear this anymore. I cannot be close to the man, but I must, for a little longer. "What do you know of the Black Hand?"

"Troublemakers, anarchists."

"Have you encountered them at all? Have you had dealings with them?" It is hard to speak. I feel unwell now. My head aches again. I sweat. I tremble. I am sure I can hear the marching and the dull crump of explosions and, weaving through it all, the relentless, ranting voice of the man in this bed. I feel dizzy. I want to be sick.

I must think. I must overcome this madness. Ever since my encounter with that wretched house, my mind has been a turmoil of strange thoughts and my head filled with voices and formless cacophony. I fight it, convince myself that it is the beginnings of a fever brought on by the day's adventures. Giving in will be the final pull of the thread that holds my body and soul together.

"Why would I?" His pain-roughened voice cuts through the turmoil and it takes a moment for me to realise that he is answering my question concerning the Black Hand. "I know them only from newspaper reports of their outrages."

"We think they are behind the attempt to kill you. It could, of course, be mistaken identity, but I don't think so."

"Am I that important?" The response is not the one I expect. *Why don't you think it was a mistake, Herr Leutnant?* would seem the logical reply, but no, the question is about himself. There is no trace of irony or humour in his voice. It seems that he means the question about his own greatness. It unsettles me, more than it should.

"You tell me," I say. An innocuous answer.

He shrugs. The act is obviously painful and makes him wince. And at that moment, in his bemused expression, in that shrug, in the oppressive weight of his presence, in the emptiness behind his fiery stare that suddenly sharpens my own sense of separation from this world, I know the truth.

Yes, I tell him silently. *You are that important.*

I recover my poise. "There is a house in an alley off the Fleishmarket, plain, three-storeys. Converted into apartments, but mostly empty. Do you know of it?"

"No. What has it to do with me?"

Always answering a question with a question. A way to gain the upper hand in conversation, perhaps?

"Are you sure you have never visited such a house?"

"Of course I'm sure. I am not welcome at anyone's house."

"Why is that?" The answer is obvious. Who would want someone like him at their table?

He doesn't reply.

I cannot bear to be near him a moment longer.

I walk away.

Thirteen

I return to the headquarters to write up a report of where I am with the case. There is no summons from Brunner. It seems as if Reiter has been true to his word and said nothing about my clumsy intrusion into his surveillance operation. Although I haven't seen Reiter since yesterday, I assume he is still watching the house, or, if the Serbians have abandoned it as a hideout, is hunting them down. Surely, otherwise he would have been back here to deliver some sort of brief. Brunner liked to be apprised of progress in all investigations—

The Serbians have not abandoned the house.

My certainty puzzles me. Then I remember that, despite his obvious terror, Nikolic returned there, unwilling but impelled by some need within himself. And Reiter, that look in his eyes, his inability to tear his gaze from the building even when angrily remonstrating with me.

A blank sheet of paper waits for me in the typewriter. The machine is a brute. It requires firm handling and does not forgive when its keys are mis-hit. I rest my fingers on the *F* and the *J*. Adela taught me to type by touch. It has saved me a lot of grief over the years. She was a stern teacher, but a good one.

It is not technique that robs me of thought, but that blank sheet of paper and my own mind, which, by contrast, is far from blank. How do I begin to explain what has happened? How do I put the inexplicable into words?

The wall of time has been fractured…he makes my skin crawl…something is wrong with…with everything when he's around.

Gibberish. The raving of mad men.

The facts. That is where I will start.

"Adolphus Hitler – resident of the Men's Dormitory in Meldemannstrasse 27 – was shot once and wounded while leaving the opera house." I add the date. "Many witnesses, but no one who can give any description of the assailant.

"Hitler's acquaintance, a petty crook who calls himself both Fritz Walter and Reinhart Hannisch, has identified Milomir Nikolic as the man who approached him for information as to Hitler's whereabouts. Information Reinhart gave willingly in exchange for money, unaware of Nikolic's intent.

"Nikolic is a known member of the Serbian revolutionary group, The Black Hand.

"I tracked Nikolic down to a bierkeller – Werner's Beirkeller – in Spittelberg. He fled before I could question him and discharged a revolver in the premises. I have since been apprised that no one was injured. I pursued Nikolic to a house off the Fleishmarket…"

…when I confronted him, I was certain that little sanity remained to him. That is where he told me that the walls of time have fractured. And the house itself…

"…I was unable to gain entrance to the house as it is already under surveillance by the Special Detective Department and I did not wish to compromise their operation." Oh, how easily the lies are imprinted on the paper. "I require a warrant in order to gain entrance to the building and arrest Nikolic."

I add brief summaries of my conversations at the Men's Dormitory and with the old man at the railway station. Adolf Hitler, difficult person, enemies made because of his argumentative and unpleasant personality, but no one knows anyone who would want to kill him.

I re-read what I have written. Dull, factual with little real content. There is nothing much more to tell. Unless I can get into that house, I have reached a dead end with my investigation. I should let it go now.

I can't and am unsure why.

Oh God, how my head aches.

"No, Leutnant," Brunner says when I deliver my report to his desk and make my request. He is trying to remain calm and even-tempered, but I can hear the exasperation in his voice. "I will not give you a warrant to search the Serbians' hideout. I will not allow you to interfere with vital surveillance. Do I make myself clear?"

Yes, he is making himself extremely clear indeed, even to me in my fogged, hungover state. I almost reveal how strange Reiter's surveillance activities have become: the fixed stares, the fear in the eyes of the detective and his men. But, of course, I withhold that particular piece of information because, surely, it would prove to Brunner that I am not fit to carry a detective's badge.

"Sir, I cannot resolve my case without arresting the chief suspect. Surely you understand this."

"You have a suspect. I congratulate you for that, but we can take no further action for the time being."

"You do not trust me, do you sir."

"What?"

"You gave me the Hitler case because you knew it was of no importance and would keep me out of your way."

"Leutnant—"

"An easy case for the damaged police officer. Why didn't you sack me instead? Orders from above?"

"No." Brunner's fist slams down onto his desk. The sound is like a hammer blow to my aching skull. "Damn it, man, you could not be more wrong. It is my superiors who wanted you gone the moment you broke down. They think you weak and no longer effective. I am the one who believes in you, Jonas. I staked my reputation, possibly my own job, on proving to them that you have fully recovered and are still the excellent officer you have always been. I needed to know if I could still trust you. I needed to know that you could carry out your duties, so, yes, an easy case. The shooting of a nondescript, probably mistaken identity on the behalf of the assailant. The conclusions of your report will be added to Milomir Nikolic's charge sheet once we have him and his associates in custody. Until then, you leave him alone. You stay away from the house. I have another case for you."

"Sir, I—"

He throws a file onto his desk and pushes it towards me. "A high-ranking Imperial Court official has received a letter threatening to expose an alleged dalliance with a prostitute. It needs to kept quiet, and the blackmailer found. I do not have to remind you how sensitive this is. Your forte, discretion and efficiency. So get to it, Leutnant Graf, and forget Heidler, Hitler, or whoever the hell he is. We have it in hand."

I snatch the file from his desk. I cannot dampen down my rage even though I know that Brunner is right and I should be grateful for the fact that he has fought for me. But my thoughts are slippery. My emotions spiralling out my control. I cannot leave this matter undone. I cannot endure the loose threads, the incompleteness, the mess.

Why not?

It doesn't matter.

Yet, it does. Christ, how it matters. It is the only way to rid myself of the nightmares and hallucinations.

The visions.

The glimpses.

From beyond the fracture in the wall of time.

"And Leutnant."

"Yes sir?

"Shave and brush your hair. Tidy yourself up. You are a disgrace to the Department. And if you report for duty with breath that stinks of the bierkeller again, you *will* be summarily dismissed. Do you understand me?"

"Yes, sir."

I slam the door to his office like a petulant child. I cannot tell him why I must get into that house. I suppose that I have convinced myself it will silence the voices and the war-sounds that rattle around inside my head. I have convinced myself that it will prove that I am fit to return to my full duties. I have convinced myself that it will remove the presence of Adolphus Hitler from my life.

In the meantime, I have little choice but to begin my investigation into the blackmail case, so I pay a visit to the official in question. The work does help to push the swirl of irrational thought and imaginings to the back of my mind, but I can summon little enthusiasm for the task. The man is small of stature but immense in self-importance. His office, his desk, his clothes, hair and moustache are immaculate to the point of obsession. He speaks in the outraged tone of the self-righteous, until I ask, politely, if he has actually visited the brothel in question. His already red moon face flares towards scarlet and he humphs an affirmative.

"Unwise for a man in your position," I say, peevishly. I am being unfair, taking out my own frustrations on this arrogant bantam. "You have laid yourself open to this sort of thing and you have threatened the security and honour of the Imperial Court." Oh, what hypocrisy. I don't care a damn about the fucking Emperor and his rotten Court. I wave towards the blackmail letter. "Does your wife know what you get up to behind her back?"

Outrage gives way to fear, and I find myself enjoying his discomfort, which is grossly unprofessional of me.

A few more questions, then a visit to the establishment concerned, where I absent-mindedly question the ladies who work there and invite their madame back to the office to look at photographs of men arrested for various moral misdemeanours. I leave her in the tender care of Sergeant Goldschmitt. The two appear to be acquaintances of long standing.

I struggle to concentrate on the case. I have already forgotten much of what the players in this sordid little drama have told me.

Because I want to go the house in the Fleishmarket. I must go. I need to go.

But I will not, because, surely, that will be giving in to the madness. Brunner is right. I need to pull myself together. I am a Police Officer. I cannot imagine ever being anything else. If I am drummed out of the Gendarmerie, then I will break down completely and probably end my life in the freezing waters of the Danube.

So I try to work, but it is almost impossible. I sort through meaningless papers. I stare at reports but see no words. The cup of coffee brewed by the ever-faithful Goldschmidt sits on my desk, undrunk. He tells me that the madame has recognised none of the faces staring up from his collection of photographs. She does, however, keep a visitor's book, a discreet tome which lists every customer and the date, time and length of their visits, as well as the name of whatever girl they spent that time with. She doesn't normally let anyone else see it, but as the good name of the Empire is in peril, she sees it has her patriotic duty to open its pages.

Tomorrow. I am in no mood for such work today.

The beat of war, its sounds and smells, march through my skull as I sit there and wait until it is dark and I can leave for home. No one cares about the attempted murder of Adolphus Hitler. No one cares that it was an execution attempt by the Black Hand.

No one cares that, for some reason I cannot fathom, the creature has latched himself to my soul and is spreading poison through my blood. I know it is all in my imagination. I'm sure that mind doctor, Sigmund Freud, would have some outlandish explanation for what is happening to me. Perhaps I should pay him a call. He lives at Berggasse 19. I know because I was in charge of the Special Detective team who watched him for the best part of a year. A waste of time. He's not a subversive or an anarchist. He's just a quack, obsessed with the sordid fantasies of the unhinged.

Restless, I watch the hands of the clock crawl through their cycle until the day fades outside and those bloody electric lights are switched on. The dark brings the terrors back. The shadows gathered in the corners of the office are no ordinary shadows, but the dark stuff that boils from those cracks in the fabric of what is real. The walls are breaking down, everywhere, all around me. The fizz and hum of the lights drill into my ears. I need to drink.

No. I must remain here for as long as I am able. I know what I want to do, but I must not.

Fourteen

This time I will not drink. I will attempt sobriety in order to protect my mind from nightmares and hallucination and not allow myself to be deluded by my own imagination. I am a damaged man. Unable to forget the human being I killed. Unable to harden my heart against the wound of Adela's desertion.

No, not desertion. Escape. She was right to run. My trauma turned me into a monster. I hadn't known until then how weak a man I am.

The temperature has dropped. The slush is freezing now and will soon be lethal to the pedestrian. I am glad to be home and yet anxious as to how I will face the hours of solitude that lie ahead.

As always, my first tasks are to light my lamps then set a fire. Comfort and illumination will help. Although I am not hungry, I force myself to eat: bread and cheese, bought for me by my housekeeper. I make strong coffee then, after selecting a book at random from the shelf, settle into my armchair. The books were left behind by Adela. I am an occasional reader; she, a habitual one. I examine the book's spine. *The Invisible Man* by H. G. Wells. A fanciful tale, and not a good choice in my present state, but hopefully it will absorb me and keep my mind from wandering into places best left unvisited.

I am stern with myself. A new leaf must be turned. A new beginning made. The investigation is over. Adolphus Hitler is no longer my concern. The case is now in the hands of Leutnant Reiter and absorbed into his pursuit of the Black Hand.

It isn't long before the need is on me, however. The need for a drink, to steady my trembling hands and still the swirl of thought. I struggle to concentrate, even though Herr Wells' story is compelling.

The house.

The damned house.

The hypnotic flicker of silver light from that upstairs window.

The dark, howling void behind the eyes of Adolphus Hitler.

My need for a drink drives me from my chair. I cross to the window, look out at the street. Darkness studded with gas lamps. A few lonely people hurry by, huddled against the cold. I envy them. Ordinary people, good people most of them, about their business. Rooted in the real world. Not plagued by mad thoughts. I feel alone up here, cut off from the world. Perhaps I should go out.

Where will I go? To a bierkeller? And what would I do there?

Drink, of course.

No, I am better off where I am.

I make more coffee, return to my chair and once more pick up the book. I stir the fire with a poker and add coal. The room is warm. Perhaps too warm. Hopefully I will fall asleep soon.

The book. Concentrate. The story is original, strange and well told.

My eyes are heavy.

I feel a hand on my shoulder. My name is whispered.

"Adela?" I look up and she is there, dressed in that white, high-collared lace blouse I know so well. There is a choker about her neck. Her fair hair is piled high, her grey eyes bright.

"The walls of time are fractured," she says and steps back.

I rise from my chair. There is darkness behind her. The lamps are on. There should be light. The darkness is liquid and swirls and writhes into awful shapes. The edges of her dissolve into it. Her gaze holds mine. She mouths words but her voice is drowned by the sound of marching feet.

I lunge for her but there is only shadow and noise. The cries of the dying, the drone of air machines, the fury of battle. I see it again, painted onto the walls of my apartment. I hear it, smell the stench of smoke, flame and burning flesh. And rising from the cacophony, that voice. The hideous ranting screaming tirade of hate and vitriol. There, a vast silhouette slamming his fist into his palm, as if beating each crazed point into his own flesh. He grows and spreads through the room. He taints the air. His presence bears down upon me until I drop to the floor and kneel and cover my ears, but his voice drills through my hands and into my skull.

Louder.

Closer.

Until the whole world is that voice.

Then silence.

It is many moments before I dare to open my eyes. My furniture, the fire in the grate, the book fallen, face downwards, onto the floor. The madness has gone, except the smell. A taint of smoke. I get to my feet, unsteadily. I glance about the room, fearful now because I know that this is no drunken nightmare. I am sober. I am awake.

This was a vision, a glimpse of what lies beyond that wall of time, and it is terrible. The horror was centred on Hitler, which seems nonsensical, because he is nothing more than an unpleasant, angry nondescript with no influence or voice in the world.

I am certain of one thing. These visions will not leave me until I find their root.

For now, however, I must drown the horrors I have seen, felt and heard. Sobriety is no longer a safe haven.

Fifteen

I am walking through the city with no memory of leaving my apartment. I remember pouring the first drink, but little more. The air out here is miserable with sleet. Great lumps of icy water splash onto my coat and hat and grind into my face. I walk in the opposite direction to my apartment, towards Fleischmarkt. I can stop, now, at any time and return home. No one has my arms. No one holds a gun to my head. Yet, I know that I cannot turn about, or prevent myself from reaching my destination. It must be faced now. There will be no peace until I find out what lies within the walls of that house and how it is connected to the loathsome creature lying injured in his hospital bed.

I reach Fleischmarkt and find myself at the mouth of a dark, narrow alley. Tenement houses and apartments line the alleyway like the faces of sheer, brick cliffs. There is no light here, other than the grey glow of illumination that leaks in from the main street.

And the silvery flicker of *that* light.

I move cautiously, aware that Reiter and his men will be concealed in some dark corner or niche.

And there it is, the house where Nikolic and other Black Hand anarchists have one of their many refuges in this city. A faceless, three-storey ugliness. The unnatural, silver light shines, shifting and uncertain, from its third-floor window.

At last. I feel an odd relief to be here, despite my fear of the place.

The silver light seems to flare brighter at my approach.

I become aware that the alleyway is not empty.

There are three figures, motionless in the middle of the road. I draw back into the shadows and wait. Oddly, the trio seem as frozen as statues. Their elongated shadows stretch out behind them and paint grotesque stick figures on the slush-dirtied cobbles. A few more seconds, then I emerge from my hiding place and, keeping to the walls, move towards the house. It draws me. The light threatens to transfix me. There are voices in my mind, ranting and screaming, that fade in and out like the signal from the Marconi wireless set our department once tried out as a communication device. I turn my attention to the three men.

And recognise Leutnant Reiter and his two loyal, thuggish detectives.

Their expressions are rapt, their eyes bright with something that resembles adoration. They seem completely unaware of my presence.

"Reiter," I say and place my hand on his shoulder. "Reiter, can you hear me?"

No answer. No response whatsoever. Nothing. I have no idea if they are even aware of my presence. Even if they are, it doesn't appear that they will make any attempt to prevent me entering the house.

I hesitate. This is the moment upon which it all turns. After this there can be no retreat. If I continue, I will have disobeyed an order and I will be, at the very least, discharged quietly from the service. My career, my reputation should protect me from disgrace or even prison, although I cannot be sure of that.

Examples have to be made sometimes, to stop others from following in my footsteps. I pause. I almost turn to leave.

A wound has opened. Perhaps it really is in the wall of time. Perhaps it is in my own mind. Whichever it is, the wound needs to be healed.

I take a breath and cross the street.

I reach the door of the house and draw my wallet of lock-picks from my coat pocket. It only takes a moment. The lock is simpler than one in the door at Berggasse 19. Yes, I entered Dr Freud's home by night and rifled through his papers and files. The Emperor's enemies are my enemies, are they not?

Inside. The darkness is complete. Even after my eyes have adjusted to it, I can see only the barest outlines and forms. A passageway stretches in front of me. There are stairs to the left of the entrance. I have no weapon. I do not know what I will do when I reach the rooms above.

I ascend, gripping the rail tightly, feeling my way up each step with my foot. My heart beats hard now. The place feels wrong, askew, as if the building has been wrenched out of true. I reach the landing.

Light. The silver-grey flicker stutters from under one of the doors on the landing. I press on. I am suddenly exhausted. My head thrums and my breath is short. My limbs ache. The house has a heartbeat… A drumbeat. There is the distant thud of explosions. The sounds grow louder with every step. They swirl about me. They press in upon me. But I grit my teeth and steel myself against them. Unseen phantom soldiers march by. Rank-on-rank. The air is filled with the drone and screech of flying machines. Children cry. Women sob.

My hand finds wide cracks in the wall as I feel my way through the flickering darkness. The cracks give entrance to unutterable coldness. And deep within those icy voids is the source of the roar and crash of battle. The sounds wax and wane, like waves that pound and drag at the sand and shingle of a beach.

I step onto the landing, then move quietly to the door of the glowing room. This is madness. There are dangerous people in this house. Anarchists. Murderers. My life could end here, tonight. Life-to-death in a moment.

The way Slavko's life was ended at my hand…

I grab the knob of the door, twist and fling it open. I freeze, waiting for the cry of shock, for the report of a gun and the unthinkable agony of a bullet blasted into my flesh…

And there is the Ghost.

It is him.

Adolphus Hitler.

He is here, yet not here. It is his image, flickering and fizzing like the electric lamps in the Special Detective Department office. It is a moving portrait that hangs in the air. A rectangle of light that holds his older, time-ravaged face and a glimpse of the room in which he sits. Its walls are dank and grey. There is the rumble of gunfire. Wherever he is, his enemies are closing in.

I become aware of the Serbians. There are three, no four, of them. One lies on the floor beside me, trembling violently, another is slumped next to him, leaning against a bed, head bowed, motionless. A third stands, hands clamped over his ears and gabbles to himself. The fourth, whom I recognise as Nikolic, kneels, staring upwards as if transfixed by the uncertain moving portrait. It looks for all the world as if these men have been driven mad. But by what? Do they hear the war sounds? Do they, like me, see and feel the cracks that tear open the walls between worlds? Yes, that must be it. Because I too want to curl on this floor, close my eyes and hide in my own madness.

"You," Hitler growls. His eyes are locked on mine. "Who...you? Why are...still sane?" His voice is scratchy and made staccato by crackles and hissing, as if played through the horn of a phonograph.

"What is this?" I try to force authority into my tone, but my voice is a dry croak. "How are you doing this?"

"A...chine. My scientists and engineers, trying... build an atomic...found...way to open the curtains of time..."

"Time?"

I can smell smoke and cordite. I feel waves of heat radiate, briefly, from the image. There are moments when I feel a tug, as if the flickering grey opening is sucking at me and at everything else in the room.

"...lost. All of it," Hitler says. "I cannot live... longer. The Bolsheviks...are closing in on...bunker... if we leave the world stage in disgrace, we'll have lived for nothing. Do...understand. Nothing. That cannot..."

"The Bolsheviks? Who?"

"The Russians, you idiot. I tried. I strove for greatness...But...betrayed...all around me...traitors, weaklings...it was so close, so near..."

"Why the Serbians?"

"...as incompetent as the rest. This must be erased. This shame, this failure, it must be erased."

The truth is breaking through. A mad, impossible truth. "*You* asked the Serbians to kill *you*?"

To murder his past self, so that the cataclysm, the war I've seen, never takes place.

"To wipe…my shame and failure from history."

My shame and failure. Even in *his* now, it is *his* legacy, *his* name at stake. Even now, at the end of a war, he expresses no grief or guilt for what he has done. God, I cannot imagine how terrible that conflict will be.

"I showed the Serbians what…to come…To their own people, by my hand. But they failed me… machine…drives men mad…must wipe away…"

The image erupts into a frenzy of hissing and flashing. I stumble back as waves of heat and cold blast outwards. Then there is a loud, white roar and I am hurled against the wall. The room fills with light.

Then there is darkness.

Sixteen

I am out and running from the alleyway in case the watching detectives gather their wits enough to storm the house, although they are still frozen in place and look unable to move, let alone storm anything.

My mind is chaos. I can still hear his voice. Whatever energies emanate from that infernal device they have infected me. My skin prickles. It feels as if I have been burned and yet there are no wounds. I board a tram. The curiosity of the few other late-night passengers is explained when I catch a glimpse of my wild-eyed, dishevelled reflection in the vehicle's night-darkened glass. My whole being feels as if it has been fractured.

I cannot still the din of war that roils through my head.

Did I become aware of those wounds in time long before tonight's encounter with that time device? Was it my proximity to Adolphus Hitler? Surely what-should-be is already altered by the attempt on his life. Perhaps it caused ripples and eddies that my torn-open soul detected? Whatever the cause, it is unendurable. I fight an urge to scream for silence. I fight an urge to press the muzzle of the revolver I stole from one of the mind-deadened Serbians against my own temple.

I pull down my hat, turn up my collar.

The revolver is heavy in my coat pocket.

I have no memory of picking up the weapon. Why had I taken it?

As before, my warrant gives me entrance to the ward, even at this ungodly hour. And there he is. Sitting up in bed. He reads. Absorbed in his book. He senses my approach and turns to watch me.

I draw the revolver from my pocket and bring it up level with his head. His eyes widen. There is fear in them now. He opens his mouth but only a groan is emitted. I can hear shouting, a scream, but they are all distant and not part of the tiny world in which I find myself.

"You…" I say. "You asked me to do this."

He shakes his head. He shrinks back against the pillows. At that moment he is a weak, frightened young man. But I have seen the truth, haven't I? I've seen what he will inflict on this world and I will never stop seeing it, hearing it, smelling its stink. I see the fragility of his skull beneath the pale, sweat-dank flesh. I see the horror in his eyes, I see the destruction I can wreak upon him. My finger tightens about the trigger. My hand trembles. I cannot do this.

The noise is loud now. No longer the sounds of combat, but one long, howling roar. It won't stop. God in Heaven, it won't fucking stop.

But.

Who am I to unravel the threads of time? What right do I have to plunge a preordained future into chaos? If not Hitler, then who or what else is to come?

I don't know what to do. Please, Christ, tell me what to do.

My breath is a series of sobs as I turn away. My arm loses its strength. I am exhausted. The gendarmes who guard the entrance to the ward are hurrying towards me. They look uncertain. I am their superior. Yet I brandish a gun.

In a moment they will act and arrest me. My life is done. My life is shattered. All for nothing.

No.

I swing back round towards the bed and its occupant. Before I can comprehend what I am doing, I level the revolver and fire. Its blast is drowned by the roar in my head.

The Ghost is a work of fiction, but it has roots in real places and events. Hitler did live in the Men's Dormitory on Meldemannstrasse 27, he did shovel snow and carry sacks of coal at a Vienna railway station, and he did paint pictures which were sold by his "friend", Fritz Walter/Reinhardt Hannisch. The Black Hand existed and were behind the assassination of Austria's Archduke Franz Ferdinand in Sarajevo in 1914, the spark that ignited WW1. I have taken liberties, of course. I am a storyteller, not a historian, travel writer, or time traveller...

AND THE NIGHT DID CLAIM THEM
by

Duncan P Bradshaw

"The night is a place where the places and people we see during the day are changed. Their properties – especially how we interact and consider them – are altered. But more than that, the night changes us as people. It's a time of day which both hides us away in the shadows and opens us up for reflection. Where we peer up at the stars, made aware of our utter insignificance and wonder, 'what if?' This book takes something that links every single one of us, and tries to illuminate its murky depths, finding things both familiar and alien. It's a story of loss, hope, and redemption; a barely audible whisper within, that even in our darkest hour, there is the promise of the light again."

Duncan P Bradshaw

"A creepy, absorbing novella about loss, regret, and the blackness awaiting us all. Bleak as hell; dark and silky as a pint of Guinness - I loved it."

—James Everington, author of *Trying To Be So Quiet* and *The Quarantined City*

blackshuckbooks.co.uk/signature